Mango Allsorts
Calm and clever;
Bambang's sun and moon.

Rocket
Stellar sausage-seek
ready for lift off.

Bambang
Daring and
devoted;
Mango's
co-star
for ever.

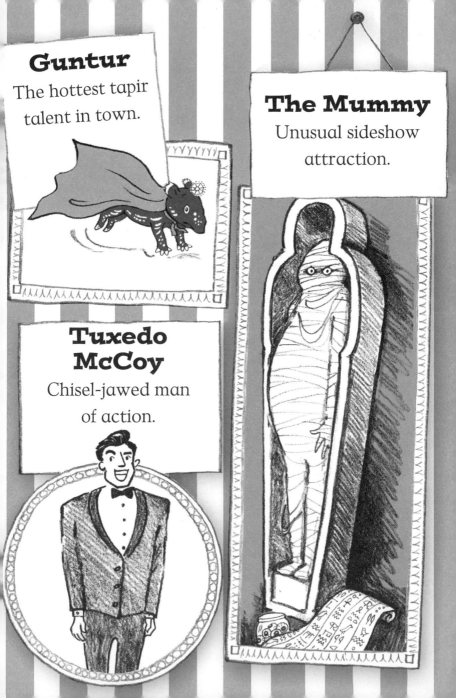

For Clara, who drew me a tapir, with love. P. F.

For Louise, with love. C. V.

First published 2017 by Walker Books Ltd
87 Vauxhall Walk, London SE11 5HJ

This edition published 2018

2 4 6 8 10 9 7 5 3 1

Text © 2017 Polly Faber
Illustrations © 2017 Clara Vulliamy

The right of Polly Faber and Clara Vulliamy to be identified as author and illustrator respectively of this work has been asserted by them in accordance with the Copyright, Designs and Patents Act 1988

This book has been typeset in Veronan

Printed and bound in China

British Library Cataloguing in Publication Data:
a catalogue record for this book is available from the British Library

ISBN 978-1-4063-7837-5

www.walker.co.uk

Mango
& BAMBANG
Superstar Tapir

POLLY FABER
CLARA VULLIAMY

WALKER
BOOKS

Contents

Snow
Day

Mango lay propped up on her elbows in bed, chewing a pencil and puzzling over her maths homework. She kept being distracted by Bambang, who was trying out new flamenco poses in her mirror. Mango wasn't sure whether the pose he was aiming for was "Tapir of Mystery" or "Tapir Full of Pie". Bambang must have been uncertain too; he stopped sticking out his tummy and turned his attention to Mango's shelf of treasures.

"What's this?" he asked, taking down a small glass bauble.

"It's my snow globe," said Mango, closing her book. "You shake it to make the snow fall." She showed Bambang

what to do and they both watched as
soft white flakes swirled around the
miniature scene.

"Ah!" said Bambang, wide-eyed. "It's wonderful." He paused, and then asked, "But what *is* snow, Mango?"

Mango thought. "That's difficult to answer," she said. "It doesn't get cold enough here to snow. Snow is frozen rain, but much better than that. It's cold and soft *and* crunchy. Everything feels fresh and different when it snows. I've only seen it once before, when I was quite little. Papa took me away on a special trip. We made a snowman and went sledging. It was fun." Mango smiled.

Bambang shook the snow globe again, watching the slow drifting flakes. "I'd like to see snow one day," he said. "I'd like to make a snow-tapir and go sledging and know just what it feels like."

"I'm sure Papa will take us both on his next trip," said Mango. "Only I don't know when that will be. There aren't many days when *all* of Papa's books are balanced." She saw her friend's face fall a little as he stared into the globe. Mango hated seeing Bambang look sad. Such a vague plan for the future *did* seem unsatisfactory.

Slowly an idea came to her. If she couldn't take the tapir to the snow, *might* there be a way of bringing snow to the tapir?

"Wake up, Bambang! Wake up! It's Saturday and it's a *special* Saturday, look!"

Bambang opened his eyes a crack and found Mango sitting on her bed, grinning at him, wearing her woolly hat and mittens. The light in the room seemed different somehow. And when Bambang looked out of the window, instead of the usual clouds and buildings, he could only see white. It was all *very* strange.

"I wanted to surprise you! I thought we'd have our very own snow day," explained Mango. "It won't be *quite* the same thing; I made the snowflakes on the window out of cotton wool and paper. But even if it isn't proper snow, we can still have fun. When you've got your warmest hat on, come to the living room."

Bambang raced to get up and ready.
He stepped through the bedroom door
and found another surprise waiting for
him: all the floor and furniture in the
living room had become white. Sheets
had been draped over everything,
creating interesting mounds. It was
difficult to tell what was a sofa or table.

Bambang paused for a moment, taking in the magical transformation.

"Come on in!" Mango stood in the middle of it all in her wellies, mittened hands outstretched.

Bambang stepped into the snow. His four feet sank down, and when he moved them it was unexpectedly noisy. *SHH-KRINCH! SHH-KRUNCH!*

"You were right, Mango!" he said. "It *is* soft and crunchy! Your snow is wonderful. How clever you are! Only it doesn't feel cold. But maybe that's a good thing."

"It's newspaper under the
sheet – that's the best I could
manage. But I've planned the
cold for later," said Mango.
"Now come and see what you
think of my snowy cushion mountain!"

Mango and Bambang spent a while
jumping and rolling off the sofa slopes.
It didn't take long for the snowy sheet
to get tangled and pulled off. Soon the
familiar colours of the furniture and the
scrunched-up newspaper on
the floor emerged.

"I think our snow's
melting," said
Bambang sadly.

"Never mind," said Mango. "How about a snowball fight?" She picked up a ball of the exposed newspaper, squished it up and threw it at Bambang. He ducked behind the sofa and started making balls of his own. They had a short but very satisfactory war.

"And now for breakfast!" said Mango when they'd both run out of ammunition. "Normally when it's snowy it's very cold outside, so you eat hot things to warm up. But I thought we'd do it the other way round, as playing in our snow has made us warm already." It was true that they were both feeling quite

flushed in their woollens.

Mango filled two tall glasses with scoops of lemon sorbet and cream soda with extra crushed ice and topped with whipped cream. She then sprinkled on large chunks of meringue and white marshmallows. "It's not a very healthy breakfast," she admitted. "But Papa agreed it should be a special occasion. It's the snowiest meal I could think of."

"It's *very* good!" said Bambang, who was cooling down beautifully with every mouthful. "It's just how I imagined snow would taste."

"And when you've finished, we've got a date with George," said Mango a little mysteriously.

Outside, it was a lovely sunny day. Mango took Bambang up to the highest point in the park – the hill where people came to fly kites or look at the view. Their woolly hats and scarves got some curious looks.

George was waiting for them. Bambang saw he had his wagon with him. It had been an ambulance when Bambang was poorly. Now it had been repainted with go-faster stripes and silver snowflakes.

"I'm calling her the Ice Queen," said George proudly. "Happy Snow Day, Bambang! Ready to go sledging?" He was also wearing a hat, scarf and gloves, teamed with shorts. But then George would have been wearing shorts even if it had been a *real* snow day.

"I *think* I am," said Bambang, feeling excited and nervous all at once.

They took it in turns to roll down the hill's gentle slope and then pull the Ice Queen back up. Just like with real sledging, the rolling down the hill took no time at all, but the pulling back up again took ages. They all got very hot.

"I'm definitely warm enough for more ice cream now. Are you still full from breakfast, Bambang?" asked Mango.

Bambang looked down at his tummy. "I could fit in another ice cream," he said.

George was facing the other side of the hill. "We could go down *that* way?" he suggested. "And squeeze in together this time. It's the quickest way to the ice cream cart."

"It's a bit steeper that way," said Mango. "It might–"

"But we're very good sledgers now," said Bambang. "Come on!"

It was a snug fit. Bambang went at the back and George at the front so he could steer. Mango was rather squashed in the middle. They began their final descent.

At first everything was fine. "WHEEEEEEEEEEE!" Their voices whipped away as the wagon-sledge gathered speed. But then, "WHEEE!" became, "AAAAAAAAAAIIIEE!" as they gathered even more.

"NOOOOOOOOOOO!"

And then became a much louder scream as they all realized they were hurtling downwards *completely* out of control.

It was an unfortunate time to
discover that wagon-sledges are not
really designed to carry two children
and a tapir. They hurtled down to the
bottom of the hill and then straight past
the surprised ice
cream seller.

KER-SPLINK!

One by one the Ice Queen lost her
wheels as they spun free and bounced
away. Now they really *were* sledging,

KER-SPLUNK!

KER-PLINK!

KER-PLOINK!

bumping and sliding along the slippery
grass, but at least, finally, they were
slowing down too.

"Watch out! We're going to crash!"
shouted George from the front. His
warning came too late. With a nasty,
wood-splitting *CRUNK* the Ice Queen
hit the low brick border
of a freshly dug
flowerbed.

George and Mango tumbled out of
either side of the wagon onto the grass,
but Bambang was catapulted up into
the air and then down onto the soft bare
earth. He somersaulted forwards and
rolled like a barrel. The gardener, who
had been enjoying a cup of tea and a
rest before she planted some marigolds,

had to run, abandoning her elevenses.

"Oh no! Oh, Bambang! Are you all
right?" cried Mango as the Bambang-
shaped mud ball finally came to a stop.
Slowly Bambang uncurled. He was
caked in earth from snout to tail, with a
marigold perched on top of his hat and
the gardener's satsuma stuck to his snout.

"I'm not completely sure. I think so," said Bambang, quivering.

"I'm so sorry, Bambang. I forgot that heavy sledges go faster," said George. He looked at Bambang and started to smile. "Were you planning on making a snow-tapir, Mango? Because..."

Mango, now satisfied that Bambang was unhurt, also began to smile. "Oh! Yes! I see what you mean..."

"What is it?" asked Bambang.

"I wish you could see yourself, Bambang! You became a mud-snow ball as you were rolling and now you ARE a beautiful, beautiful, mud-snow tapir!"

"Am I?" said Bambang, looking down to his feet and squinting at his snout curiously. "Why, *yes*! I suppose I am. How clever of me!"

Bambang gave himself a shake. Mango and George sheltered from the flying earth behind the remains of the Ice Queen. Then they handed the muddy marigold and satsuma back to the gardener with an apology and went to pick up the lost wheels. Finally they bought their ice creams.

The three friends walked slowly through the park, licking their cones.

"I think," said Bambang, "that I'm

not all that sorry that it doesn't usually snow in the city. I think I'd rather eat cold than walk in it."

"True," said Mango.

"But I'd still like to see snow fall," said Bambang. "I'd like to stand in my very own snow globe and catch flakes with my snout."

Mango looked up and smiled. "Do you know, Bambang, I think you *might* even get that wish granted."

Standing by itself on the grass was a tree. Its wide branches arched and hung low, heavy with white blossom. The heat of the day had been relieved by a cool breeze, which was lifting petals from the flowers. In gentle swirls they were drifting down and gathering in piles on the ground below. It did look rather like Mango's snow globe.

Mango, Bambang and George stood under the tree. They let their heads and shoulders get covered in the delicate flakes of white.

"It's tickly!" said Bambang. "Like my feather boa." He swished his feet through one of the soft piles, then lay down and rolled from side to side.

"You're making a tapir snow angel, Bambang!" said Mango.

Mango and George lay down too, and moved their arms back and forth to make their own angels. Then the three friends were quite still, their heads together as they watched the pattern the falling petals made for a long, long time. And although not a single real snowflake had fallen, all of them knew that nobody and no tapir could *ever* have had a snowier day.

A Night
at the Fair

Many more newspaper snowballs were found around the apartment in the weeks after Mango and Bambang's snow day. One even found its way under Mango's papa's study door, distracting him. He picked it up, ready to put it in the bin, and then paused. Perhaps there were things other than books that needed to be balanced?

He smoothed the ball out and smiled.

ALL THE FUN OF THE **FAIR!**

for one night only!

When Mango got back from school
that afternoon she found Bambang
waiting by the front door and Papa *out*
of his study. They had a plan to skip
book balancing, homework, clarinet and
flamenco practice for the evening. Papa
was taking them to the fair.

The sun was sinking below the city skyline as they arrived at the fairground. The lights on all the rides were being turned on, and flashing, wheeling rainbow spots and stars filled the sky. The music boomed and there were throngs of people. Everywhere smelled of hot sugar and popcorn.

Mango's papa, freed from the weight of

his books, seemed as floaty and carefree as a let-go-of balloon. He said Mango and Bambang could go on as many rides as they liked. But Bambang, a little overwhelmed, wasn't sure at first how many he *would* like.

"Perhaps I'll just watch you, Mango?" he said, staring up at the big wheel in alarm.

Mango turned Bambang away from the biggest rides and took him towards one of the gentler ones. It was a merry-go-round with lots of different vehicles.

"Look Bambang," she coaxed. "Wouldn't you like to sit in that lovely bright fire engine and ring its big brass bell?"

Bambang was reassured by the number of quite small children on the merry-go-round already. He agreed he *might* like to drive a fire engine and squeezed in. Mango chose a motorbike and the ride began. Bambang saluted Mango's papa with a clang of his bell on every circuit.

Clang!
Clang!

"That was a *lot* more fun than I
thought it would be," said Bambang
as he and Mango got off, a little dizzy.
"Let's do that one now." He pointed to
the spinning teacup ride.

After that there was no stopping them. They went on the waltzer, the dodgems *and* the Octopus, one after the other. After the last, they were wobbly in legs and tummy and hoarse from screaming, but both grinning broadly.

"Shall we go on the rollercoaster?" asked Mango, but here Bambang drew a line. The plunging railcars looked too much like their recent sledging experience for comfort. Instead, Mango's papa bought them both bags of candyfloss *and* toffee apples, and he promised he would win them prizes on one of the side stalls.

"Are you going to bang the hammer down hard enough to ring the bell at that strongman stall?" asked Mango, teasing Papa a little. But Papa would not be teased, and replied seriously that in his younger days he *had* been considered something of a master at the hoopla. He fancied trying his luck on that stall again.

So Mango and
Bambang stood to one
side and ate their toffee
apples and candyfloss
while Mango's papa
bought three rings to
throw. And, slightly
to Mango's *and* the
hoopla stall owner's
surprise, Papa threw
the first ring around a
small china cat, which

he presented to Mango, the second around a flashing bow tie, which he gave to Bambang, and the third around a box of bright silk handkerchiefs, which he pocketed himself.

Mango cheered and Bambang drummed his feet – because his mouth and snout were busy with sugar – to show their appreciation.

The star prize on
the stall was a teddy
bear about the same
height as Mango. It
was far too big
to throw a
ring around,
so to win it,
all *three* hoops
had to be thrown

around the very furthest peg, which
was positioned at an awkward angle
at the back of the stall. Mango's papa,
buoyed by his success, decided he would
now attempt this additional feat. He
purchased three more rings.

"It's quite a large teddy, Papa," said Mango. "I'm not sure where we'd put it." But Papa was determined. His first two hoops landed over the peg, but the third missed. Having got so close, Papa bought another set of rings.

Frustratingly, these three fell wide too. Mango's papa put his hand in his pocket to buy another go. Mango, who had finished her toffee apple, felt fidgety. She guessed that Papa wouldn't stop playing now until he won. She looked around the other stalls.

"Papa, would you mind if Bambang and I went and explored that tent over there while you keep throwing?"

At the edge of the fairground Mango saw a striped marquee with a board outside it.

ANCIENT TREASURES OF THE MUMMY'S TOMB REVEALED!

ENTER AT YOUR OWN RISK. PAY THE MUMMY OR SUFFER THE MUMMY'S CURSE!

Mango's papa gave her some coins.

"Come on, Bambang!" said Mango. "We learned about ancient Egypt at school. I'd like to see the treasures."

Bambang was less keen. He didn't like the sound of mummies or curses. However his toffee apple and candyfloss were causing more immediate difficulties. His teeth had been gummed together by the toffee, which made conversation difficult, and the candyfloss was wrapped round his snout in a tickly, sticky mess.

"Mmmmnnn-wraha-mmm," he said as Mango disappeared into the tent. Bambang had no choice but to follow her in.

It was very gloomy inside the tent. In the middle of the space was an upright sarcophagus. Its gold lid, covered in mysterious hieroglyphs, had been propped to one side. A stiff, bandaged figure was revealed within, staring out with black-hole eyes. Next to it was a wooden box with a slot for coins and a sign reading:

PAY THE MUMMY! NO TOUCHING.

Around the base of the sarcophagus were the promised "treasures". They were not quite what Mango had expected. There were a few jars and pieces of papyrus, and a mummified cat. But there were also odd things that didn't seem likely to be that ancient at all: a glued-matchstick sphinx, the face of Cleopatra made out of breakfast cereal and a matted wig labelled **TUTANKHAMUN'S HAIR**. This last still had a shop label attached.

Tutankhamun's hair

100% NYLON

"I suppose it was too much to expect real treasure, but this is just silly. I thought it might at least be a *real* mummy. That model isn't at all convincing. It looks more like a bandaged over-stuffed scarecrow," said Mango. "Oh well. Come on, Bambang. Bambang? What is it? What's wrong?"

"MNNNN-MMMMMN-WRAHA-WRA-MMMNN- NNN!" said Bambang. He suddenly froze, wide-eyed and panicked-looking. He stared at the mummified cat and at the mummy, then started to back quickly out of the tent. But before he could get there–

"SILLY indeed! OVER-STUFFED SCARECROW, you say! You two AGAIN!"

The mummy spoke! It stepped out of the sarcophagus and began to walk forwards. It held a quivering bandaged finger outstretched. "PREPARE TO MEET YOUR DOOM! I CURSE YOU!" The voice was familiar...

"Oh!" squeaked Mango.

"YES!" said Bambang, finally free of toffee and able to speak. "Unusual things, Mango! I've seen that cat before, Mango! RUN, Mango!"

But the mummy was already stumbling towards Bambang, arms reaching and bandaged hands grabbing him. "HA! GOT you! You SHAN'T escape!"

Bambang found his snout clasped in a firm grip. He wriggled and squirmed. Mango looked desperately for something other than Tutankhamun's hair that she could use to attack the mummy.

But Bambang's snout was still covered with candyfloss. Sticky with it, in fact. As he pulled and twisted, Mango saw the bandages around the mummy's hands begin to loosen and unravel.

"That's it, Bambang! Pull! This way!"
Mango opened the flap of the tent to
make space as Bambang fell backwards,
bringing the mummy out with him. The
pressure around his snout was relieved
as the grasping hands lost their grip. Free
at last, Bambang charged off blindly into
the crowd, an attached bandage
streaming behind him.

The mummy was pulled into a spin on the spot as the material quickly unravelled. Passers-by gasped and covered their eyes; who knew what horrors might be beneath?

Mango had a pretty good idea. As the final bandages fell away, she found herself facing her dizzy, red-faced and *very*-angry-indeed ex-neighbour. It appeared that Dr Cynthia Prickle-Posset, Collector of the Unusual, wanted by the police for artefact theft and smuggling, had been uncovered.

"YOU and that BEAST destroyed my museum! My LIFE'S WORK! And now you TRAMPLE my NEWEST collection!" The trail of cereal-crumb footprints and broken matches suggested that both the sphinx and Cleopatra had been a victim of Bambang's panic. "Now I will be AVENGED. If I can't have the beast, *you* will be REMOVED once and for EVER!"

Suddenly Cynthia Prickle-Posset grabbed Mango tightly around her middle, lifting her right off the ground. Mango, taken by surprise, kicked and struggled but Cynthia Prickle-Posset, who would have done well at the strongman stall, started carrying her back towards the tent.

"How dare you! What do you think you're doing? Put me down!" said Mango, trying to wriggle out of Cynthia Prickle-Posset's bandage-free and worryingly secure grasp.

"I should ALWAYS have dealt with YOU first. MEDDLING child. My CURSE will be a SECURE boarding school, VERY far away. You'll be QUITE invisible transported in my SARCOPHAGUS. NOBODY shall find you."

Mango felt small and unusually helpless. She needed Papa and Bambang, and she needed them now. Where were they?

"Hel–!" She tried to shout but Cynthia

Prickle-Posset clasped a hand over her mouth, muffling her cry. They were almost back inside the marquee.

"OW!" said Cynthia Prickle-Posset suddenly, and then, "OOF!" and "AI!" Three hoopla rings hit her hard on the head one after the other. She loosened her grip and Mango broke free.

"Oh Papa!" cried Mango, running

into her father's very tight squeeze indeed. "And Bambang!" she cheered a second later.

Bambang charged straight into Cynthia Prickle-Posset, knocking her to the ground and tangling her in mummy bandages.

He pinned her down with his feet. Now it was the Collector's turn to struggle.

"No one but NO ONE collects our Mango!" said Bambang, fierce with love and worry.

But the mummy had one last curse to deliver. Cynthia Prickle-Posset took out her scorpion-shaped hairpin and thrust it hard into Bambang's tummy. Poor Bambang cried out and sprang up immediately, and Cynthia Prickle-Posset was able to scramble to her feet and get away.

Mango's papa shouted, "Somebody stop her! Police!"

But the Collector ran into the darkness beyond the fairground.

"Bambang!" cried Mango, running over to her friend. His wound, although deep, thankfully did not appear life-threatening. Papa hurriedly opened his new handkerchiefs to help staunch the bleeding. By the time Bambang had received the first aid he needed, it was too late for them to pursue Cynthia

Prickle-Posset. The Collector had escaped once more. Mango, Papa and Bambang were too relieved to care.

Once the immediate drama was over, Mango's papa sat down rather heavily and wiped his forehead with his one remaining silk handkerchief. He muttered something about being a careless fool who would never allow himself to be distracted by hoopla again.

"But Papa! That would be a great mistake!" said Mango. "I know you didn't win that teddy. But you saved me! And there wouldn't have been room for it *and* Bambang anyway.

You are definitely the most masterly hoopla master that ever was. Your aim was *very* careful. Thank you!"

"Winning Mango back was the best prize of all," agreed Bambang. "Although I love my bow tie," he added politely.

Mango and Bambang helped Papa to his feet. And then he bought them one last treat: hot chips and hot chocolate to make everyone feel better.

They ate them as the end-of-the-fair fireworks exploded, lighting up their faces and the way home. All three of them felt they had experienced enough "Fun of the Fair" to last a long, long time.

Rocket
to the
Moon

It took a few days for Bambang and Mango to recover from the shock of their encounter with the mummy. They sat together in Mango's cupboard with a tin of biscuits, taking it in turns to wear Bambang's hats.

Even Mango's papa
needed an occasional
session with the Very
Brave Hat. Only after a

conversation with the police was he
reassured that Cynthia Prickle-Posset was
unlikely to be troubling them for some
time. The police had received reports
about a stowaway who matched her
description on a research ship carrying
fresh supplies for the scientists studying
penguins and icebergs in Antarctica.
The boat would be away for months.

Mango and Bambang could only feel sorry for the scientists who would find a bad-tempered Collector delivered unexpectedly with their tins of baked beans, sardines and peaches.

Bambang's wound healed quickly, although he was left with a small scar. His friend Rocket was *very* jealous when he felt brave enough to go out and show it to her. "A scar! How brilliant! You're so lucky! I didn't get anything *half* so good from the fair. There were tasty pickings around the hot-dog stall and the bins, but the space shuttle ride was a *terrible* swizz! All it did was go up a bit and then round and round!"

Bambang had forgotten how interested in space travel Rocket had become recently. One afternoon, Mango had invited Rocket to come for tea after a play in the park. They'd all watched *Woofy: Pup Space Cadet!*, a cartoon about an astronaut dog. Rocket had been transfixed and had sat unusually still for the whole programme. After that she'd thought and talked of nothing else. But then she'd always had a thirst for adventure.

"*I* could be Woofy – the first dog on the moon! Wouldn't I be good at that, Bambang? A proper explorer! I've seen the world – now for the stars!"

Bambang was supportive of Rocket's dream, but baffled. He felt himself to be very much a cling-to-the-earth-with-all-four-feet tapir, although he was sure there was nothing his friend couldn't achieve if she wanted to.

A few days later he found Rocket in the park, squeezing an old goldfish bowl over her head. She explained her plan.

"Look, Bambang! I'm ready for blast-off! I just need a bit of extra bounce. You can help! Sit down hard on the end of that see-saw and I'll stand on the other end. If I jump as I go up in the air I'm bound to get high enough! I'm a really springy jumper!"

Bambang had a feeling that even the downward thrust of his bottom was not going to be enough to get Rocket to the moon, but he didn't want to dampen her enthusiasm. They counted down from ten and he gave it the best go he could. Rocket *was* launched ...

but only as far as the park's bed
of newly planted marigolds.

Rocket got up, still cheerful. The flowers looked a little less happy.

"Oh well! Looks as though I will need to hitch a ride on that new spaceship after all." Rocket looked over in the direction of the city skyline and wagged her tail. "They must have been waiting for me before blasting off! Don't worry, fellow space-explorers, I'm on my way!" She turned back to Bambang. "See you soon my friend! Look out for me on the

moon and I'll wave! Can't wait to try moon sausages!" Then Rocket trotted off.

Back at home, Bambang shared his worries with Mango. "She said she was going to take a spaceship. She seemed quite certain she knew of one. But I don't think she's thought about all the different aspects of space travel – her helmet didn't look very safe. I'm not sure it's really like the one on *Woofy*."

Mango tried to make Bambang feel better. "I'm sure she'll be back in the park tomorrow for more games, Bambang. There *are* no spaceships here. And even if there were, Rocket wouldn't be able to stow away on one unnoticed."

But although Bambang looked in all the usual places in the park, there was no sign of Rocket the next day. Or the day after that. He asked all the dogs if they'd seen her. He was even brave enough to make enquiries at the pound. Everyone shook their heads; everyone knew Rocket and no one had seen her.

That evening, Bambang gazed out of the apartment window at the glowing disc of moon above. He strained his eyes, willing the speck of a jumping, wagging shadow to magically appear on its surface. Mango stood at his shoulder and looked too.

"Wherever Rocket is, I'm sure she's all right Bambang. She's very good at looking after herself, isn't she?"

"Oh, yes. Only, I have this lump. It's somewhere just above my tummy and below my throat. It's a not-knowing-worrying sort of lump. I don't normally have it when I think about Rocket adventuring, but I do this evening," said Bambang.

Mango knew about that lump. She'd felt it herself in the past when Bambang had been in trouble.

She pulled Bambang's ears gently. "OK. I'll help you look in the

morning. I hope we won't have to
go to the moon to find her!"

The only clue they had to help
their search was Rocket's claim that a
spaceship was ready and waiting for
her in the city. "Could she mean one of
the exhibits in the Science Museum?"
suggested Mango. They were walking
the city streets showing Rocket's picture
to passers-by.

"I wouldn't have thought so. Dogs aren't allowed in there. It's *very* unfair," said Bambang. He was trying to sniff out Rocket's trail with his snout. He kept catching whiffs of possible leads and then finding they led to pizza stalls and rubbish bins instead. These were things that Rocket normally smelt of, so the confusion was understandable.

"I know. I would be *furious* if there were signs like that put up about tapirs... Oh, wait a minute – hang on Bambang – what about–?" Mango suddenly stopped and pointed. They were in the busiest, tallest section of the busy city. Just across the road the

city's shiniest new skyscraper was being built. It had been growing floor by floor over the last few months and was nearly complete. An immense tier of scaffolding snaked up one side. Cranes were lifting concrete blocks and steel beams while teams of builders laboured in hard hats.

But it was the poster on the boarded front of the building that had attracted Mango's attention.

There was an artist's impression of what the finished building would look like – all silver and shiny and tapering off into a smooth point in the sky. Mango and Bambang looked at each other in excitement.

"*The* Rocket for our Rocket, do you think? With the scaffolding still up and all the shiny surfaces, it really does look like it's about to take off," said Mango.

"Yes! It looks like Woofy's rocket," said Bambang. "Rocket must have seen it. We *have* to get inside and check, Mango."

DANGER

Mango and Bambang hurried over to explain the problem to one of the hard-hatted builders.

But he just laughed. "The agent only takes *serious* buyers up for viewings. Not random children and animals with a shaggy-dog story!"

Bambang's lump of worry hardened. He started to argue with the builder. "Rocket's not a *shaggy* dog..." he began, but Mango led him away.

"If they only take serious buyers up, then that's what we'll have to become, Bambang." She put on a pair of dark glasses. "I'll do the talking." They went round to the temporary cabin office marked "Sales".

"Good afternoon," said Mango in her most dignified voice to a man at a desk inside. "My client here would like to view the Penthouse right away, please. He's a *very* busy tapir."

"Eh?" said the agent. Bambang quickly adopted his best Tapir of Power and Influence pose.

"I can't say too much," continued Mango, "but his connections are far-reaching. He's looking for the perfect home to match his position and create the right impression. Money no object."

"Um..." said the agent.

"You'll have seen the cover of this month's *Hollywood Star* of course? A young relative of my client. In fact my client taught Guntur *everything*," said Mango, scooping a magazine off a pile on a coffee table in a moment of inspiration. It had a picture of Minty Verbena and Bambang's cousin on the front.

"Oh yes – of course I know *Guntur*!" said the agent, more impressed. "But the Penthouse is unfinished. It's been locked off-limits since the concrete floor was poured a few days ago. Perhaps your client," the man nodded at Bambang, "could come back in a week?"

"A week!" Bambang couldn't help exclaiming. "We can't wait a week! That might be too late!"

The agent had never met a tapir before but Bambang's expression and sense of urgency seemed to impress him. It had been a slow day and he wasn't going to turn down the chance of a quick sale. "Well ... if you don't mind quickly viewing it from the lift in its unfinished state, I suppose I can take you up."

The lift was a temporary one within the scaffolding – open air and rickety. Going up in it, all wearing helmets and jackets, was a bit too much like being launched into space for Bambang's comfort.

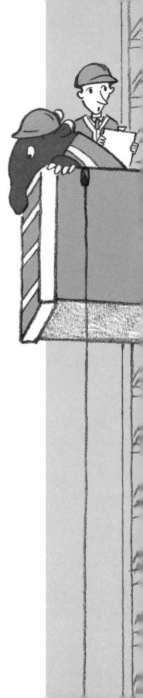

AROOOOO

But as they neared the top of the building, where the walls were only half finished and the windows were still missing, a lonely sound steadied his resolve. They all heard it: a desolate, whistling howl.

"The wind makes a very interesting noise this high up, doesn't it?" said the agent. "Of course all we'll be able to do is get a sense of the space and the views from here. We can talk about fixtures and fittings and take a deposit back in the office. Here! What are you doing? Where are you going? Wait!"

But Bambang couldn't wait. As the lift reached the final floor and its gate opened he bounded across the still-wet floor. Familiar footprints trailed across the concrete. Bambang followed them desperately. He searched inside a gold-topped bathtub, waiting to be plumbed in, and a pile of builder's sand. Finally, behind a stack of breeze-blocks, he found the source of the lonely howl. Rocket, still in her helmet, was curled up and shivering. Bambang picked up the grubby and tired space traveller lovingly. She was looking even smaller than usual, especially about the ribs. He carried her back to Mango and the surprised agent.

Rocket wagged her tail weakly
as Mango lifted her helmet off. She
managed a small lick of Bambang's
snout and then flopped.

"I *almost* made it to the moon, see
Bambang?" she said. "Only there were
no sausages. No sausages at all. And
then I couldn't get back down to Earth."

A few days and *very* many Earth sausages later, Mango and Bambang went and queued for a safer trip to space. Mango was carrying a bulging rucksack on her shoulders and hoping nobody would notice that it occasionally wriggled. The Planetarium was another place with unfair notices about dogs.

ABSOLUTELY
NO DOGS
OF ANY KIND
WHATSOEVER

Once they were safely inside and
in the dark, Rocket came out of the
rucksack. She was wearing a special
Moon Dog medal that Bambang had
made her. And then Mango, Bambang
and Rocket leant back on their seats,
looked up and took flight together.
They didn't only stop off at the moon,
but visited the planets, stars and outer
galaxies as well – travelling even
further than Woofy.

"Thanks for the trip, but I think
I'll stay on Earth for the time being,"
Rocket said to Bambang when the show
was finished. "I like the way it smells.
There's enough to keep me busy."

Bambang was very relieved to hear it. And he decided he *wouldn't* mention the new series that had just started on television – *Dodie the Deep-Sea Merdog* – just in case it gave Rocket any other ideas.

A Tiny Tapir's Tears

The thick, gold-edged card had been sitting on the mantelpiece for a week. It was very exciting.

You are invited to the international premiere of
"TEARS OF A TINY TAPIR"!
Starring MINTY VERBENA!
Introducing GUNTUR as the Tiny Tapir!
Champagne and canapés. Black tie.

A signed photo had been included with the invitation with a note scrawled on the back: "Darlings! Mini-G and I jetting in for this! Know my poppet would love to see you! Kisses XX."

"But we don't have any black ties," Bambang had fretted.

"It just means wear your smartest clothes," explained Mango. "You can put on your bow tie from the fair if you like. *And* your Special Occasion Hat!"

Bambang was pleased about that. Very few occasions were special enough for his Special Occasion Hat. He was delighted to have a chance to show it off. It would give him the confidence to face Guntur, his small tapir cousin, who could sometimes be a little squashing. This would be the first time he had seen

Guntur since his move to Hollywood to live with Minty. He took a long time getting ready.

"Oh it's you. What *are* you wearing?" Guntur said to Bambang when they met on the long red carpet outside the cinema. Excited crowds had gathered to watch the limousines pull up and to get autographs from the celebrities

inside them. Camera flashes exploded as photographers called out to famous people to smile. Guntur, sporting gold-painted toenails, a silk cape and a diamond earpiece that didn't look like it had come from the hoopla stall at the fair, galloped up and down the carpet. He waved his snout to his fans, blew raspberries and posed for picture after picture.

Minty Verbena, in an elegant gown, stood by a microphone and held up her hand for quiet. "Darlings!" she said. "Darling Guntur and I are so thrilled and *humbled* to be here with you to introduce our first movie together! I do hope you've brought your hankies!" She blew kisses. Guntur dived under her skirt and pretended to be shy, with just his soft snout

and button eyes peeking out. There was a collective "Aaaah!" from the crowd. Then he popped out and galloped around some more.

"It's a totally brilliant film because I'm totally brilliant! Lucky you!" he said. The crowd laughed warmly. Minty Verbena turned and went into the cinema, Guntur trotting at her heels. Close by on her other side was a startlingly handsome man with a chiselled jaw and luxuriant hair.

"That's Tuxedo McCoy," whispered Mango to Bambang. "He mostly does Westerns, but I think he's in this film too."

They followed the stars into the cinema and were shown to seats at the back.

The lights were dimmed, and with swelling piano music, the movie began. The titles opened with a full-screen shot of Guntur's face, his eyes brimming with tears; then the camera panned back to reveal the whole of him, huddled in a dark doorway at night, a blizzard blowing round him. "He's been in real snow!" whispered Bambang.

The film had many twists and turns. Guntur played a starving orphaned tapir, who was adopted by Minty, uncovered a smuggling ring and recovered a locket showing Minty to be a long-lost heiress. Then they were both kidnapped. They were rescued by Tuxedo in a dramatic finale involving a train and a lot of running and shooting.

"What a silly story," said Mango as the lights came up at the end. The audience around them were applauding and cheering.

"I suppose so," said Bambang, who had been hooked throughout. "Guntur was terribly clever and brave though, wasn't he?"

"But that wasn't *really* Guntur. He was acting, Bambang. It was all just pretend," said Mango.

"I suppose so," said Bambang again. He wasn't sure it made a difference. He couldn't help feeling once more that his cousin was a very superior sort of tapir to himself.

They were shown into another part of the cinema for the party. It was a crush of fashionable people talking and laughing and drinking champagne. They all seemed to know each other.

Mango and Bambang stood to one side, not quite sure what to do. Mango found them glasses of pink lemonade. Bambang was excited about the canapés on giant silver platters but was disappointed to discover they were just normal food, made too small.

Guntur was in his element. He jumped
on top of a grand piano in the middle
of the room and ran up and down the
keys, giggling. As Mango and Bambang
approached, Guntur flagged down a
waiter and began polishing off an entire
platter of mini cheese puffs. "Hello! Have
you come to tell me how brilliant I
am too? Everyone's saying
so," he said, spitting out
cheesy crumbs.

Bambang *was* a little star-struck. "I was hiding under my seat when you bit the smugglers. *And* when Tuxedo swung you and Minty onto the train from the broken rope bridge! And when you were lost in the blizzard! You were so daring!"

Guntur looked down his snout at Bambang from his vantage point on top of the piano. "I know. Other tapirs don't have half my talents. I'm *very* special. I'm daring enough to do EVERYTHING."

Mango frowned. "I'm sure you are, Guntur," she said. "But I think perhaps you had a stunt double as well? And made the film on a set, with the special effects like the snow added afterwards? Guntur wouldn't

have been in the slightest bit of *real* danger, Bambang. Not like when you and Papa rescued me and you got stabbed..."

Guntur looked sulky. "Well, I *could* have done all my stunts myself, but Minty said I was far too valuable to risk it. The studio's insured my snout for over a million dollars."

On the other side of the room Minty Verbena tapped the side of her champagne glass to make a speech. Tuxedo McCoy was by her side; his hair gleamed and his spectacular teeth sparkled under the light of the chandelier.

"Mini-G! Where's my darling Mini-G?" called Minty. Guntur jumped down from the piano, brushed past Mango and Bambang and trotted through the crowd. Minty picked him up, planted a lipstick kiss on both his cheeks and addressed the party.

"Darlings! A teeny-tiny announcement! I know I once *seemed* to have it all: fame, beauty, riches, a star on Hollywood Boulevard and a cabinet full of awards..."

There was applause. "But darlings! If you only knew. My heart was empty. It all meant nothing, *nothing* until my darling Guntur found me and brought the sunshine!" Minty, her eyes brimming with crystal tears, pressed her cheek against Guntur's. He gave her a small lick. She put him back down on the floor. "Mini-G, you were the first to teach me how to love. Now I am so happy to share the news that *more* love has followed! Because this evening my *other* co-star, darling Tuxedo, has asked me to marry

him. And, my darlings, I've said YES!" Minty turned, beaming, to Tuxedo and he clasped her in a tight embrace while the room cheered.

Not *all* the room was cheering though. Mango nudged Bambang. "Look at Guntur." Guntur was frozen, watching the newly engaged couple. His face reddened, his cheeks puffed out and his button eyes turned stony.

WAAAAAAA

"Oh dear," said Bambang, recognizing the signs. Suddenly the tiny tapir exploded with a wail. Minty and Tuxedo stopped embracing.

"Mini-G? What *is* the matter, darling? We're going to be *such* a happy family," said Minty.

AAAAAAH!

But Guntur, over-excited and over-tired, was spoiling for a not-so-tiny tantrum. "You're not to marry that man. You're *not* to. You belong to *me*!" He rolled on the floor and kicked all four of his legs in the air. He thrashed and howled.

The noise went on and on. Nobody seemed to have any idea how to stop it, until Mango grabbed a champagne ice bucket and emptied it over Guntur's head. The wailing stopped abruptly and Guntur sat up. Water dripped down and puddled around him.

"Think I don't dare do my own stunts?" he yelled. "I'll show you. I'll show everybody! Watch this!" Guntur jumped up onto a chair and then ran across a table, made a wild flying leap and grabbed the chandelier. He began to swing back and forth

Hi-YAR!

on the light fitting, dangling
upside down on his back legs.
With a cry Guntur
swept over Tuxedo
McCoy's head. His
million-dollar snout
snatched hold of the
star's thick, glossy locks
and pulled. The crowd
gasped as Tuxedo's
thatch of hair came
off in one neat
sweep.

Guntur dropped the wig on top of a waiter's platter of elaborate small jellies.

"Darling!" cried Minty.

"Varmint!" shouted a red-faced Tuxedo, turning stony-eyed himself. He rolled up his sleeves menacingly.

Bambang felt like he was watching a whole new movie – one that might not be heading towards a happy ending. But while most of the party were looking at a shiny-headed Tuxedo climbing on the table and trying to grab

CRACK

a giggling Guntur, Bambang suddenly noticed another danger. A jagged looking crack had appeared on the ceiling where the chandelier was attached. The added weight of the not-quite-tiny-enough tapir seemed to be more than it could take. The crack was spreading with alarming rapidity.

"Quick, Mango!" Bambang said. "Grab a tablecloth!" The two of them hastily swept up a rectangle of white linen and held it outstretched under the chandelier. Tuxedo made a lunge for Guntur but his arms grabbed the air. Mango and Bambang had just got into position when, with a CRA-ACK and a terrified tapir scream, chandelier and ceiling came down together.

The room disappeared in a cloud of plaster and dust. There was coughing and confusion and Minty's cries carried over the top: "Guntur! My Guntur! Not my DARLING!" Her anguish was heartfelt.

Mango answered her. "It's OK, Minty. We've got him. He's fine, I think. Bambang

was just in time." As the dust settled, Guntur's head popped up from the makeshift net that had caught both him and the chandelier. He trembled from the shock of his fall, and suddenly looked very tiny. He started to cry; neither the movie droplets nor tantrum theatricals of before, but real tears that left him puffy-eyed and rather snotty about the snout.

"Want my Minty," he said. "Need my Minty."

"Oh my heart! My precious, precious Mini-G." Minty swept over and clasped him to her. "You are a naughty tapir. But my darling I do love you so. Never frighten me like that again."

"I won't, Minty. Sorry Minty," said a chastened Guntur.

"And darling! Say thank you to your darling cousin and his friend! So brave and quick-thinking! How will we ever repay them?"

"Thank you Bambang," said Guntur, very, very quietly. "And Mango."

"That's quite all right," said Bambang, suddenly feeling big-cousinly and not so inferior after all.

Tuxedo had been reunited with his hair. He was looking slightly less murderous, but as he came over to join them Mango judged it might be a good time to give the new family some space.

"The film and the party have been a lovely treat but Papa will be waiting for us," she explained. She and Bambang headed for the exit, although not before Minty had issued an open invitation for them to come and stay in Hollywood –

"Any time darlings!"–and a big cheese producer had given Bambang a card with his number on it.

"Tapirs are so hot right now," he said. "Call me."

Outside, Bambang took off his Special Occasion Hat. It had been pinching a little. "Big food is better than small food," he said, thinking again about the disappointing canapés as his stomach rumbled.

"I think so too," agreed Mango. "And I also think big tapirs are *much* better than small ones." She gave Bambang a squeeze.

"Really?" said Bambang. He looked at her sideways. "All of them?"

"Well I was thinking of one in particular," said Mango. "Although maybe that one will be tempted to run away to Hollywood and get his snout insured for a million dollars now?"

"Oh no!" said Bambang. "He'd be very silly to do that. Not when there's snow and fireworks and even trips to the moon here. Not when there are friends in general and one very much in particular. This tapir definitely prefers real life. That is–" Bambang had to check to be safe– "if you mean *me*?"

"I do mean you," said Mango, smiling.

"I thought you did," said Bambang. "Good."

And just like the end of all the best movies, the two friends strolled off into the sunset. And, with a few more adventures along the way, it's quite possible that they lived happily ever after.

Also in the
MANGO & BAMBANG series

The Not-a-Pig

Tapir All at Sea

Tiny Tapir Trouble

"All the elements of a classic"
Literary Review